THIS BLOOMSBURY BOOK

BELONGS TO

....

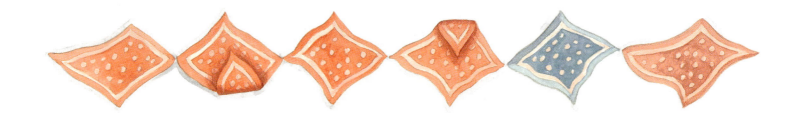

Imagine a town, in a country, where a simple thing like an Elephant had never been seen, or even heard of …

Well, not so long ago, there was a town exactly like that, and one day the people awoke to find an Elephant sitting bewildered in the main square, mopping his brow with a red spotted handkerchief and wondering how he got there.

At first the people were afraid of him. But he seemed so friendly that they soon lost their fear and went over to speak to him out of curiosity.

'What's your name?' they asked. 'And what are you?'

'I don't know,' said the Elephant. 'And I haven't got a name, and I don't know what I am.'

The people all looked confused. How could a thing as big as that have no name? And not know what it was?

'You've got no business not to have a name,' they said.
'You've got no business not knowing what you are!'
'I know what he is,' said a little boy who was seven and three quarters and known locally for telling Tall Stories. He told them he'd seen bears on the moon! His name, (and it was his name because it was embroidered on either sock) was Eric, and no one ever listened to him.

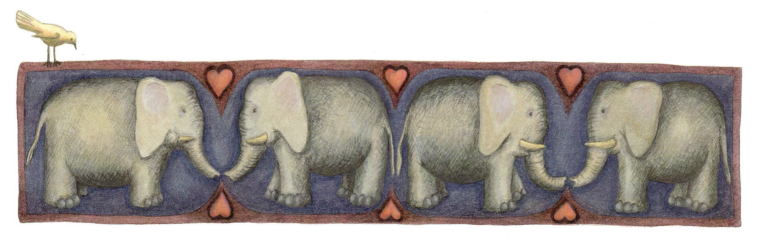

'I know exactly what he is!'

'Quiet,' said the Policeman. 'I'm going to poke him with this stick and
see what he does.'

The Policeman poked him and, as expected, the Elephant didn't like it.

'Maybe it wants plugging in?' said someone. 'Wants wiring up?'
'He's not electric,' said Eric.
'Look at that nozzle on him,' someone said, 'what's that for?'
No one knew, except Eric, and no one was listening to him.

'All right, I've got it.' said the Train Driver. 'It's obvious what it is. It's a new type of railway engine.'

So they took the Elephant to the railway station and connected him to a train. But he wouldn't move.

'Why doesn't he go?' asked everyone. 'Give him some coal.'

'But I don't like coal,' said the Elephant. 'I like buns and cakes.'

'If you like buns and cakes,' said the Train Driver, 'then you can't be a train. I wonder what you could be.'

'I'll tell you what he is,' said Eric.

'Oh, do be quiet!' said various grown-ups.

'All right, it's obvious what he is,' said the Fireman. 'He's a fire engine. Look at his hose! That's what that long nozzle is. Give him to me, I'll put a fire out with him.'

So they took the Elephant to a fire and pointed him at the flames. But he didn't like it at all, and was frightened of the red and yellow blaze.

The people of the town were very proud and pleased with their
Elephant, so pleased they built him a special house and garden in the park
with a greenhouse to grow his vegetables — (melons, carrots, cucumbers)
— which the Professor discovered was his proper food.

'Thank you for my lovely house,' said the Elephant to all his guests at the moving in party. 'But if you wouldn't mind, there is one more thing I would like?'

'You can have anything,' they said. 'What is it?'

'A name,' he replied.